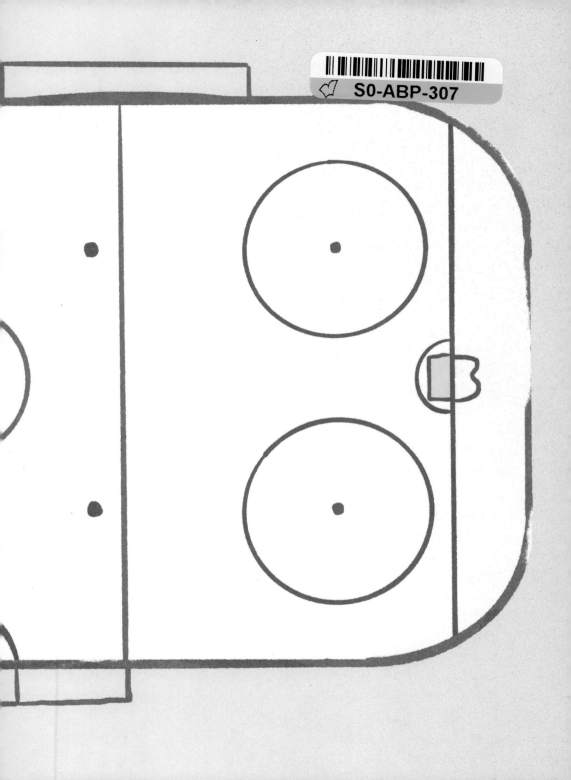

This book series is special to our family. The books teach real life lessons and the joys of hockey, family, and teammates. Hockey Day is a special holiday to all of us in Minnesota. We love these books!

—*Matt and Bridget Cullen*
Three-time Stanley Cup champion

I'm a big fan of books that teach kids about hockey and more importantly about the value of accepting those who may be different and working together as a team. It's important to lead by example and treat everyone with the same respect.

—*Claude Giroux*
Captain, Philadelphia Flyers

Keep reading, keep skating, and keep making new friends. That's what life is all about.

—*Rick Nash*
Former NHL player, Boston Bruins

This book has great lessons kids everywhere! I'm so happy my good friend Ann and the American Special Hockey Association can be an inspiration for so many people!

—*Alex Ovechkin*
Captain, Washington Capitals

This book teaches real life lessons through sport, through victory and losses, and emphasizes the importance of hard work regardless of score.

—*Jocelyne Nicole Lamoureux-Davidson*
Olympic gold medalist, Team USA

A fun story that shares the love of family and hockey!

—*Corey Perry*
NHL All-Star, Dallas Stars

Like all Minnesotans, we vote yes for Hockey Day and treasure the friendships hockey gives to all players! Keep reading!

—*Phil and Sen. Karin Housley*
Hockey Hall of Famer

I might dye my beard red, white, and blue for special hockey! Special hockey rocks! Reading is important! Do it!

—*Brent Burns*
Defenseman, San Jose Sharks

It's super cool playing hockey with my friends. I love skating, meeting new friends, and cheering for the Caps! A book about hockey, the Ice Dogs, and my dream of being the Capitals announcer is a hat trick of awesomeness!

—*Ann Schaab*
Washington Ice Dogs

I love the way this book celebrates individual differences, strengths, and similarities. When children learn about themselves, others, and the world around them, that is the ultimate hat trick.

—*Aimee Jordan*
Lila's mom; advocate for people with disabilities

Hockey is more than a sport—it's a culture. And the best part of hockey's culture is that it continually brings friends together.

—*Avery Hakstol*
Daughter of NHL coach Dave and Erinn Hakstol

DROP THE PUCK

IT'S HOCKEY SEASON

JAYNE J. JONES BEEHLER

ILLUSTRATED BY CORY JONES

Whitaker Playhouse

IT'S HOCKEY SEASON

ISBN: 978-1-64123-664-5
Printed in the United States of America

© 2021 by Jayne J. Jones Beehler
www.officialadventures.org

Illustrated by Cory Jones

Whitaker House
1030 Hunt Valley Circle
New Kensington, PA 15068
www.whitakerhouse.com

1 2 3 4 5 6 7 8 9 10 11 **WJ** 28 27 26 25 24 23 22 21

DEDICATION

To the many hockey players in our lives, past and present,
who shared their passion, love, and spirit of the game.

A NOTE FROM JAYNE

I promise you will fall in love with *Drop the Puck*, this series of books about two brothers, Cullen and Blaine. They love hockey and each other. We have included a glossary in the back to help you understand new words in the book and learn more about hockey.

Blaine was born with Down syndrome and has special needs. Down syndrome is a genetic disorder that can cause physical growth delays, certain facial features, and mild to moderate intellectual disability.

At times, Blaine's speech can be stuttering, slurring, and repetitive. It might be challenging to read and understand at first. But don't give up. Blaine wouldn't—and you shouldn't either! As you read, ask your parents and friends if you need help. You can also talk to us at chris@officialadventures.org.

7

AND THE STORY GOES—
     FOR THE LOVE OF THE GAME.

PREGAME: BREEZERS AND JERSEYS

It was the day after Thanksgiving. Delicious dinners of turkey and fixin's were done. For many, it was a day of shopping and reminiscing about their traditions and family gatherings.

Most people's tummies were still full. But for anxious and energetic hockey fans, there was still room in their tummies for a few butterflies to flutter. The biggest and best Thanksgiving tradition remained—another reason for giving thanks. It was the holiday tournament and the launch of the long-awaited hockey season!

Rylee the Referee grabbed his phone and texted his reffing partner, Rosee. "U ready to rock it, Ref. Rosee? C U at the rink in 10. Don't forget your whistle!" Ref. Rylee grabbed his skates, whistle, and bag. He headed out the door.

As the snow fell lightly outside, young skaters tucked their brand-new jerseys into their breezers. They laced up their just-sharpened skates. And they all awaited the crisp sound of the puck-drop to salute the start of the season!

Hockey moms and grandmas settled on the bleachers. They were covered head to toe in toasty, warm blankets. They sipped hot chocolate to help keep the chill away.

Proud dads gathered, greeting each other with high fives and handshakes. Each one tried to cheer louder than the others to show how pumped up they were. The competition began before the puck even dropped.

"The blood's in our g-game, and the g-game's in our blood," sang Blaine as he jammed to his favorite song on his headphones.

Looking at his younger brother, Cullen tried to hide behind his overstuffed hockey bag. "Mom, can't you do something? No one pumps up to 'The State of Hockey' song!" Cullen smiled as he let out a good-natured groan.

"Oh, come on. I think every Minnesota hockey player does! You pump up for games to your favorite song," their mom replied. "You know Blaine is just as fired up as you. He might have Down syndrome, but that surely doesn't get him down!"

"Yeah, but Blaine's just the team manager. Filling water bottles and taping hockey sticks is nothin' like scoring a hat trick every game." Cullen winked.

"He might not be scoring goals on the ice, but he's scoring goals in the game of life!" Mom reminded him.

"Let's play hockey!" shouted Ref. Rylee as he walked into the rink. He grabbed Blaine into a hug and Blaine grinned. "It's great to see you back at the rink, Blaine. I need to go find Rosee, your other favorite referee. We'll see you on the bench! And don't you even think about squirting me with a water bottle. But squirting Ref. Rosee is fair game." Ref. Rylee winked and walked away.

"I g-got a hug from R-Rylee the Referee," Blaine bragged to Cullen.

"Settle down, little bro! It's time to head over to the bench and get your manager work done. We need to win this tourney. And hugging the referee doesn't help score goals." Cullen laughed.

"N-no. But it might help…k-keep you out of the penalty box!" joked Blaine.

"Really? In that case, Blaine, you better go get a hug from Rosee the Referee too!" Cullen joked back as the brothers shared their traditional pregame laugh.

Without skipping a beat, Blaine snapped his headphones back on with a smile. His voice rang out, "Innnn the state, the state of hockey, hockey!"

The smooth sheet of ice glistened under the arena lights. It was resurfaced and ready for the action. Players huddled up close to the rink boards. They got a last-minute boost from their coaches as they waited for the referees to join them on the ice.

Cullen looked up to the bleachers. He saw all the parents carefully positioning their cell phones to take photos of the game, the team, and their favorite players.

He thought to himself, "Our parents and families are the best fans." His family didn't miss a game. Half of his mom's pictures would probably be action shots of Blaine on the bench. Cullen couldn't wait to see what pictures she took today. When they got home, he'd post them to social media and show his friends what they were missing.

2

PERIOD ONE: WHISTLES

"Yeah! Woot, woot. W-woot!" yelled Blaine. He clapped his hands as Ref. Rylee skated by the bench.

Ref. Rylee did a quick snow-spraying stop. With a grin, he asked Blaine, "Hey, man—you ready for this game?"

Nervous to talk, Blaine slurred, "Yes, yes, y-yes, *sir*." He carefully organized the team's sticks in order of height and checked the water bottles.

Ref. Rylee praised him. "You are the best hockey manager in America," he said.

"I know!" Blaine laughed.

Ref. Rylee drank from the team's water bottle and then squirted the ice.

"Hey! Watch how much you squirt—I fill those up!" Blaine tried very hard to reply with little slur or interruption. "I love being the t-team manager. And I love hockey!"

"We all do, Blaine." Ref. Rylee smiled in agreement. "Best game in the world!"

As Rylee put down the water bottle, Ref. Rosee skated over. She picked up the bottle. As fast as Rosee could, she squeezed it at her reffing partner. Ref. Rylee jumped and shrieked at the unexpected shower, giving Blaine an instant belly laugh.

Blaine's mom was secretly positioned behind the bench with her phone. She snapped a quick shot of Blaine laughing at the referees' water fight.

"You ready to get this tournament started?" Ref. Rylee asked Blaine. Rylee put his whistle to his mouth.

"I was ready last week! Let's play hockey!" Blaine stated as crisply and proudly as he could.

"You got it, coach." Rylee winked at Blaine.

Ref. Rylee blew his whistle, ordering the face-off. He pointed to both goal judges, readying them for action. He dropped the puck quickly and skated backward, out of the way.

Instantly, parents began rooting and screaming from the bleachers. There was a bright flash of light on the ice from all the phones taking pictures. Players on each bench joined in with shouts of support.

"Come on, boys! We got to pass the puck," encouraged the coach.

Cullen's team struggled throughout the first period. His team had no shots on goal in the first eight minutes, while the other team had sixteen! Cullen and his teammates were frustrated and impatient. They all knew that no offense would mean no tournament championship trophy.

Blaine clapped louder and louder in the bench area, watching every play. As players returned to the bench after each shift, Blaine patted the tops of their helmets in a show of support.

"Hey, quit smacking our helmets! Leave your hands off my teammates," snapped Cullen. He pointed to the corner of the bench. "Go sit over there!"

Confused by his brother's reaction, Blaine sat quietly on the bench for the rest of the period.

"Knock it off, Cullen," yelled the coach. "Don't take your frustration out on Blaine."

The coach turned to the whole team gathered at the bench. "You all need to start playing the puck. You need to focus on getting goals in the net! We each have a job to do on this team. Blaine is doing his best. He showed up to play and win! Now, the rest of you need to join him and step up and do your job!" Coach said this all in one breath.

Cullen knew his coach was right. He had taken his own frustration out on his brother. But that didn't make him any less upset. The game wasn't going well at all. Not only was there no offense, but he and his teammates couldn't stay out of the penalty box. The entire team needed to play harder and create scoring chances.

3

FIRST INTERMISSION: WATER BOTTLES

The game was scoreless after the first period. Blaine quickly gathered all the water bottles to fill them. In the locker room, the team sat quietly.

As Cullen walked in, he slammed his stick against the wall in anger. Instantly the stick snapped, broke into three parts, and flew across the locker room.

"C-cool your j-jets!" Blaine yelled as he went to pick up the pieces of the stick.

"Gentlemen…" Coach paused and took a breath before he continued. "You have a job to do, and that's to play hockey as a team. Pass the puck, play your positions, and get that puck in the net."

The coach began to walk out of the locker room. But first, he pointed directly at Cullen. "You owe your parents a hundred dollars for that stick! Get your head back in the game!"

After the last bottle was filled, Blaine roared loudly, "We got this! Go score a g-goal!"

"Get outta here, Blaine!" Cullen shouted at him. He stood up and pointed to the door, ordering Blaine to leave the locker room. "You're just the manager—you're not a part of this team!"

The other players didn't say a word. A heavy silence fell in the locker room.

Blaine's forehead wrinkled and he bowed his head. He gathered the water bottles as quickly as he could. With his arms filled up with empty bottles, he walked onto the freshly cleaned ice. Overloaded and moving too quickly on the slick ice, Blaine's feet slipped out from under him. Water bottles flew into the air and onto the ice.

Blaine's mom jumped up and started down the bleachers. But as she stepped toward the ice, she saw Ref. Rylee skating quickly over to Blaine. She instantly stopped and watched.

"Need a hand?" Ref. Rylee asked, reaching out to Blaine.

Blaine just shook his head. He tried not to let Ref. Rylee see the tears welling up in his eyes. Rylee reached closer anyway, and Blaine grasped his hand, slowly getting his footing again.

"No goals yet in this barn burner," Ref. Rylee said. He looked at Blaine and saw the tears. "Hey, what's going on, champ? Cat got your tongue?" he joked, trying to get a smile.

"My, my…t-team doesn't like me," he answered.

Ref. Rylee laughed out loud.

When he realized Blaine was serious, he stopped laughing. "Not a chance, Blaine," he said. "You are the heart of this team. You know it, I know it, and they all know it." Rylee pointed to Cullen and the team coming out of the locker room. "Chin up, and get back to work," he said to Blaine. "You have a game to win!"

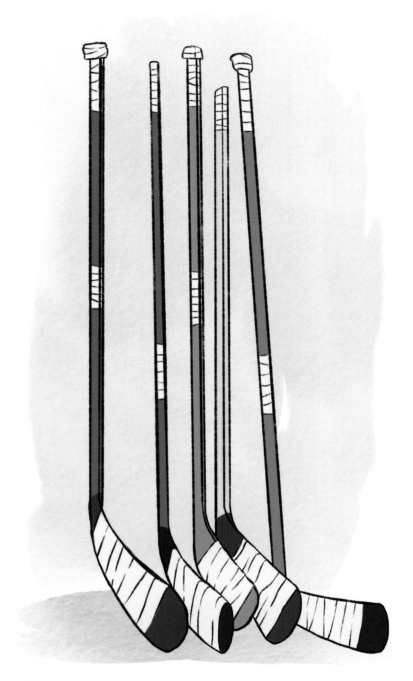

4

PERIOD TWO: HOCKEY STICKS

Players from both teams took to the ice for the second period. Ref. Rylee skated one last circle, passed the team bench, and reached out to give Blaine a high five. But Blaine wasn't on the bench. Rylee saw the team's water bottles lined up perfectly and filled to their brims. In the corner, the team's hockey sticks were taped, ready, and precisely positioned. So where was Blaine?

The second period didn't go much better for Cullen and his team. Unfortunately, Cullen didn't bring a new attitude onto the ice either. Instead, he sat in the penalty box for the majority of the second period. From high-sticking to tripping, Cullen didn't play fair, and he wasn't a good teammate.

His mom took plenty of photos of his record-setting penalty minutes.

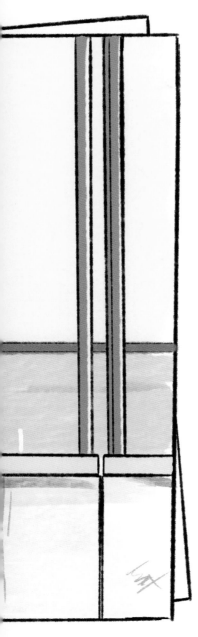

"It might not be the best memory, but it's certainly a memory we'll never forget," she said to his dad as he came up to the bleachers.

His dad laughed and exclaimed, "We'll remember it as the Thanksgiving tournament where Cullen sat the entire second period in the penalty box!"

"It takes all kinds of record breakers to make hockey history!" Cullen's grandpa joked.

"Don't go making hotel reservations for Cullen's induction into the Hockey Hall of Fame just yet!" his mom added with a laugh.

"You gotta love hockey," his dad said. "It teaches lessons beyond just winning. Speaking of winners, does anyone know where Blaine ran off to?"

"I think he went back into the locker room," his mom answered.

The horn blared throughout the rink. The second period had come to a close. And Cullen's team had yet to score a goal.

5

FINAL INTERMISSION: PAINT CANS AND PAPER

Cullen and his teammates swung their sticks against the ice in frustration and headed to their locker room. As Cullen glided past Ref. Rylee, he threw down an empty water bottle and shot it like a puck.

Ref. Rylee picked up the water bottle and looked at it closely. The bottle was wrapped with hockey tape. On the tape, a handwritten message read, "The only disability in life is a bad attitude!" Rylee smiled to himself, knowing exactly who wrote it. He wondered if Blaine had written a message on every bottle.

"Why do we have a team manager if he can't even fill up a water bottle?" Cullen said with obvious frustration.

"The best hockey manager in America," Ref. Rylee began, "wasn't on the bench for the second period."

"I'm sure my brother is just off pouting," Cullen snapped.

"I don't think he's the one pouting." Rylee pointed out. "You could learn a lot from Blaine about hockey and life."

"He doesn't know anything about hockey," Cullen shot back as he headed for the locker room, swinging his stick in a hissy fit.

When Cullen kicked open the locker room door, he could not believe his eyes. His teammates stopped and stared right along with him.

There sat Blaine in the middle of the locker room, surrounded by cans of paint and pieces of poster board.

The team huddled around Blaine to read his posters. Together, the posters spelled *T-E-A-M*.

"W-where did you get the paint?" asked Cullen when he could finally speak.

"Mom, b-brought it," answered Blaine.

The locker room erupted in cheers and laughter. And the teammates all gathered around Blaine in a circle of fist bumps.

"Am I p-part of the team now?" Blaine asked Cullen.

"Part of the team?" Cullen echoed. "You should be wearing this C for captain—not me." Cullen tapped his own chest.

He patted his brother on the head with his gloved hand, just as he would for a teammate. "I'm sorry for being mean to you. Ref. Rylee is right on. You are the world's best brother and hockey's favorite manager!"

"Thanks, Cullen," Blaine answered through a widening grin.

6

PERIOD THREE: PILE OF HATS

Ref. Rylee skated over just in time to see Cullen patting Blaine's head as they came out of the locker room. "Who's got one last period of hockey in them?" Rylee asked with a grin.

"For the love of the game, we all do!" Cullen cheered.

"Best game in the world!" crowed Blaine in agreement. He set up the *T-E-A-M* posters behind the bench.

Ref. Rylee looked at the posters and then smiled over at Cullen. "Yep, I think Blaine understands hockey just fine!"

47

With renewed spirit, Cullen and his teammates took to the ice. Every swipe of the stick, every crack of the puck seemed to happen in perfect rhythm. Before long, the horn blared, bringing the third period to a quick close.

Cullen had scored a hat trick, and the team won their first game of the season! Cheering families filed down from the bleachers, taking pictures of the team and the final score on the scoreboard.

"That was the most exciting period of hockey I've ever seen!" Grandpa shouted.

"Where did that sudden spurt of energy and team spirit come from?" Mom asked.

"I'd like to announce today's star team member," the coach said as the parents and players gathered around. "Congratulations, Blaine! You didn't give up on the game or give up on the team. Your energy, spirit, and positive attitude shined through and helped us win this game!"

"Way to go, bro! You deserve it!" cheered Cullen. He and the rest of the team picked Blaine up and lifted him high above their shoulders.

"C-careful...you don't want to drop today's...MVP!" Blaine giggled.

49

ASK THE OFFICIALS
RYLEE AND ROSEE'S REFEREE RESOURCES

Important Words to Learn

assist: An assist in hockey is credited to up to two players of the scoring team who shot, passed, or deflected the puck toward the teammate who scored the goal.

attitude: A feeling or a tendency to respond positively or negatively toward a certain idea, object, person, or situation. Attitude influences your choice of action.

barn burner: An extremely exciting hockey game or competition.

body checking: Knocking an opponent, sometimes against the boards or to the ice, by using the hip or body.

breezers: Pants worn as part of a hockey player's uniform.

championship: A competition held to determine a winner.

Down syndrome: A genetic disorder that can cause physical growth delays, characteristic facial features, and mild to moderate developmental disabilities.

goal: A goal is worth one point in hockey and it is valid when a puck passes over the goal line and into the opposing team's goalie net.

hat trick: When one player scores three goals in one game.

Hockey Hall of Fame: A hockey museum dedicated to celebrating the history of ice hockey. It holds exhibits about players, teams, records, and trophies.

official: The main on-ice referee whose job is to determine penalties and award goals during the game. The official uses hand signals to enforce fair rules of the game.

penalty: A punishment for breaking the rules of the game. Most penalties are enforced and served by a player within the penalty box for a set number of minutes, during which the player cannot participate in play. Penalties are called and enforced by the referee.

penalty box: The area where a player sits to serve the time of a penalty.

resurfaced: To clean dirty, rough ice with an ice machine to make fresh, smooth ice.

stuttering: To speak or utter with an irregular repetition or drawing out of sounds.

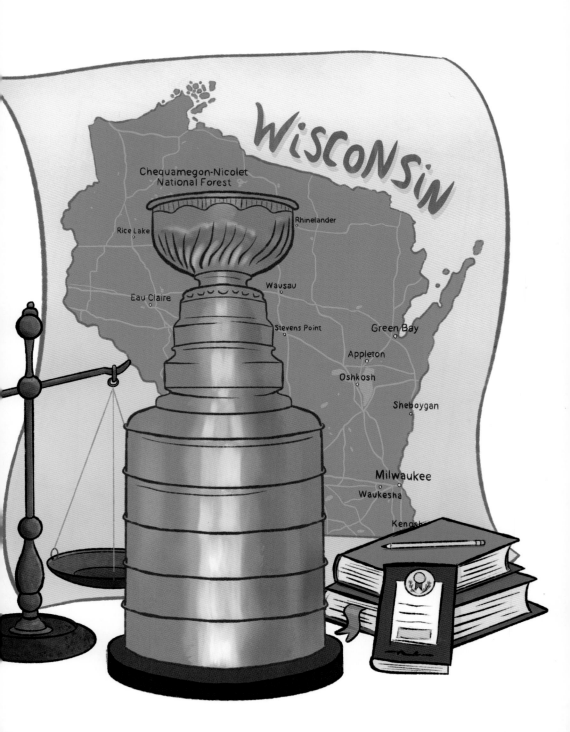

MEET JAYNE

Jayne J. Jones Beehler wears many helmets, including hockey sister, college professor, lawyer, author, wife, mother, advocate for children with disabilities, and lifelong hockey fan. She's also a former live-in nanny who can never have enough children or chaos around her. Jayne resides in Florida with her husband, a hockey coach and former goalie. Every night, there's a game on their TV! Together, they founded a chaperone travel nonprofit organization to ensure that individuals with developmental disabilities can travel independently.

www.officialadventures.org

TALK TO THE AUTHOR

Jayne would love to talk with you about the Drop the Puck book series! You can email your questions to her, share your favorite hockey stories, send her your best hockey photos, or just drop by to say hello. Write to Jayne at Jayne@officialadventures.org or find her on social media.

You never know! Jayne loves to incorporate real inspiring kids and hockey stories into her book series. Plus, you can score some awesome Drop the Puck prizes!

GAME DAY DECISIONS

- Describe your favorite part of this book.

- Was there anything in it that surprised you?

- If you could be a character in the book for one day, who would you chose to be and why?

- Imagine you are a Hollywood director and you're going to make a movie based on this book. What would you do?

- If one of the characters could come to your house for dinner, who would you like to invite?

+ Describe this book in one word. What makes you choose that word?

+ How did the setting of the story affect the characters?

+ Were there any new words that you learned from reading this book?

+ What do you think the author wanted you to take away from this book?

+ Have you ever been to a special hockey ice practice?

+ What makes hockey so awesome?

OTHER BOOKS IN THIS SERIES!

AVAILABLE WHEREVER
CHILDREN'S BOOKS ARE SOLD!